RABBIT & BEAR

Rabbit's Bad Habits

STORY BY
JULIAN GOUGH

ILLUSTRATIONS BY
JIM FIELD

Silver Dolphin

Silver Dolphin

Silver Dolphin Books
An imprint of Printers Row Publishing Group
A division of Readerlink Distribution Services, LLC
10350 Barnes Canyon Road, Suite 100, San Diego, CA 92121
www.silverdolphinbooks.com

First published in Great Britain in 2016
by Hodder Children's Books

Printers Row Publishing Group is a division of
Readerlink Distribution Services, LLC.
Silver Dolphin Books is a registered trademark of
Readerlink Distribution Services, LLC.

All notations of errors or omissions should be addressed to Silver Dolphin Books,
Editorial Department, at the above address. All other correspondence (author
inquiries, permissions) concerning the content of this book should be addressed
to: Hodder Children's Books, Carmelite House, 50 Victoria Embankment,
London, EC4Y 0D, UK

ISBN: 978-1-68412-588-3
Manufactured, printed, and assembled in Shenzhen, China.
First printing, September 2018.
RRD/09/18
22 21 20 19 18 1 2 3 4 5

As the robber left the cave,
he stood on Bear's nose. Bear
woke up.

"My honey! My salmon!
And my delicious beetles'
eggs!" said Bear. "Gone!"

But outside, in the snowstorm, there was
no sign of the robber, or the food.

Snowstorm? thought Bear.
SNOWSTORM?! This isn't Spring...
I've woken up early! Oh well. I've always
wanted to make a snowman.

The storm ended.

Bear rolled a snowball all the way down her hill, and up to the top of the next. She sat down, panting.

"It's the end of the world,"
said a gloomy voice.

Bear looked all around. "No it isn't," said Bear cautiously. "It's a lovely sunny day."

"Nonsense!" said the voice, from below. "The sun's gone out."

Ah, thought Bear. She rolled
her snowball sideways, and
uncovered a rabbit hole.

Rabbit popped out. He
looked at Bear. He looked at
the giant snowball.

"Only an idiot," said Rabbit thoughtfully, "rolls a snowball *up* a hill..."

"Why?" asked Bear.

"Gravity."

"What's Gravity?" said Bear.

"Gravity," said Rabbit rather importantly, "Is the Mysterious Force which Attracts Everything to Everything Else."

"Ah!" said Bear, nodding.

"Like friendship."

"No!" said Rabbit.

"Love?" asked Bear.

"No!! No!!" said Rabbit.

"Oh...hunger?" said Bear, who was feeling mysteriously attracted to the idea of breakfast.

"No!!! No!!! No!!!" said Rabbit, and shoved Bear's giant snowball as hard as he could. It rolled down the hill, faster and faster, getting bigger as it went, and skidded across the frozen lake until the ice cracked. Bear's snowball disappeared...

with a

PLOP

Bear's mouth opened in shock. "See?" said Rabbit triumphantly. "Gravity WANTS you to push snow DOWN a hill, and will help you. But gravity does NOT want you to push snow UP a hill, and will try to stop you. And only a fool," said Rabbit severely, "picks a fight with gravity."

Bear finally closed her mouth, sighed, and began to roll another snowball. "You know an awful lot about gravity," she said.

"I am an expert," said Rabbit. "Gravity nearly killed my grandfather. Now, if you could do me a favor..."

"I'd be delighted," said Bear.

Rabbit nodded. "Go away," he said. "And take your avalanche with you."

"What," said Bear cautiously, "is an avalanche?"

"An avalanche," said Rabbit, pointing at the snowball Bear was rolling, "is a huge load of snow that rolls down a mountain faster than a train. My grandfather was buried in an avalanche. He had to eat his own leg to survive, while he was waiting for them to dig him out."

18

"Really?" said Bear, impressed. "He must have been buried for a very long time."

"Well, no," said Rabbit. "About ten minutes. But he was very hungry. We get VERY, VERY hungry in our family."

Bear's stomach rumbled.

"Oh yes," said Rabbit.
"I forgot. You don't have
any food."

"How do you know?"
asked Bear.

But Rabbit was gone.
He soon reappeared.
"No hard feelings," said
Rabbit. "Here." And he
handed Bear the oldest,
saddest, floppiest,
blackest carrot Bear
had ever seen. "You can eat
it. Or use it as a nose for your
snowman."

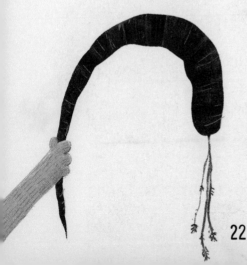

22

Bear sniffed the black, floppy carrot. Ugh. "Er, nose, I think…" said Bear. "Would you like to help me build my snowman?"

Rabbit thought for a second. "No," he said.

Bear sighed, turned, and
rolled her snowball back down
Rabbit's hill. By the time she'd
got it back up her own hill, it
was bigger than the first one.
Perfect, thought Bear, panting.
She started to make a head for
her snowman. Pretty soon she
was singing.

In his burrow, Rabbit could hear Bear's songs.

"Hmm," said Rabbit. "Making a snowman DOES seem to be..." Rabbit had trouble saying the next word, because he'd never used it before. "F...f...f...f...fun...Hah! I shall make an even BETTER snowman." But first, for energy, Rabbit ate lots and lots AND LOTS of the honey, frozen salmon, and delicious beetles' eggs that he'd stolen from Bear during the storm.

Then he did a little poo, and ate it.

This rather embarrassing habit
was the reason Rabbit never invited
people over for lunch.

"I forgot to say thanks
for the carrot," said Bear's
voice, right behind Rabbit.

"Aaarkk!" Rabbit jumped
his own height in fright
and scrambled out of the
burrow. "Oh. Bear...You're
welcome..."

"By the way, Rabbit, did you just eat your own poo?" asked Bear, wondering if she'd seen right.

"Ah," said Rabbit. "Yes. A little bit."

"A little bit of YOUR OWN POO?" asked Bear, wondering if she'd heard right.

"Shush!" said Rabbit, glancing around. "Look, all rabbits do it. It's perfectly normal."

"For a rabbit, maybe," said Bear.

"Well," said Rabbit, drawing himself up to his full height, which gave him a good view of Bear's tummy, "I'm sure bears do some things in the woods that they wouldn't like to talk about."

34

"But WHY do rabbits eat their poo?"
asked Bear.

"Well, why do YOU eat?"
said Rabbit.

"Um, to get energy.
And to make new
bits of Bear."

"Exactly," said Rabbit. "It's easy to make a bear out of honey, salmon, and delicious beetles' eggs. They're full of energy. It's easy to make a wolf out of meat. FULL of energy. But it's really, really difficult to make a rabbit out of plants."

"Why?" said Bear.

"Because when you've eaten the plants, and digested them in your tummy for hours, and pooed them...the job is only half done!"

"No energy?" said Bear.

"None!" said Rabbit. "The energy is still trapped in the poo! It's sort of soft and black, like licorice..."

"Yes, yes," said Bear hastily.

"So you have to eat your own poo," explained Rabbit, "and digest it ALL OVER AGAIN, to get the energy out."

"Really?" said Bear. For some reason she wasn't hungry any more.

"Yes," said Rabbit. "And THEN you have to poo a totally DIFFERENT kind of poo...sort of a dry, brown poo, with just the grassy, twiggy bits..."

Bear felt a little weak. "So, um, er...do rabbits eat the other kind of poo?" she said.

"What?" said Rabbit. He couldn't quite believe his enormous ears.

"The dry brown ones, with the grassy twiggy bits," Bear added helpfully.

"Eat the other kind of poo?" said Rabbit. "EAT THE OTHER KIND OF POO? That's DISGUSTING!"

"Oh good," said Bear. "Just checking."

"From dawn to dusk, you're eating and pooing," said Rabbit gloomily.

"And half the time you're eating poo. It's an awful life."

"Maybe that's why you're so grumpy," said Bear.

"Grumpy?" said Rabbit. "I'm not GRUMPY!"

"OK, you're not grumpy," said Bear. "Well, I'm off to, er...wash my carrot."

45

I hate being a rabbit, thought Rabbit, as he climbed down into his burrow to eat more of Bear's food.

Then, full of energy, Rabbit got back to
work on his snowman. Soon he had rolled
a huge snowball right over his burrow.

"What a lovely little head!" shouted Bear from her hilltop. "Thanks! But I've already made one!"

"It's not a head," said Rabbit, furious. "And it's not for you! It's a body! I've only started! And it'll be much bigger than yours! Eventually!"

Bear gasped.

"Why," said Rabbit, irritated, "are you gasping? Don't you believe me?"

"I am gasping," shouted Bear politely, "because you are about to be eaten by Wolf."

Rabbit looked over his shoulder.

Wolf was bounding across
the snow toward him.

Gosh, Wolf had a lot of teeth.
And Rabbit's snowball blocked his burrow.

"Aaaarrk! Splfff!
Waaahhh!" exclaimed Rabbit,
and turned and ran...

51

Oh dear, thought Bear. Rabbit gave me a carrot...so he's my friend...

Bear made a snowball and
threw it with all her strength. It
went over Wolf's head and landed on the
frozen lake. Crack. Plop. Whoops...

Bear made a second snowball, and threw it, with a lot less of her strength. It only fell a few feet in front of her.

Bear frowned. She made a third snowball, and threw it, with just the right amount of her strength. It landed on Wolf's head, right between his ears.

THUD!

Far below, Wolf skidded to a halt,
shouted, "You keep out of this!" to Bear,
and raced on again after Rabbit. Bear
sighed. No, to stop Wolf you'd need a
snowball as big as an avalanche,
and as fast as a train...
Hmm. Wait.

Bear knocked off her
snowman's head, and
sent it rolling down the
hill, toward where Wolf
was going to be in about
a minute.

Bear was actually a
lot cleverer than she
thought she was.

Rabbit, as he ran, looked over his shoulder at Wolf, and his eyes opened wide.

"Look behind you!" gasped Rabbit.

"I'm not falling for that," panted Wolf. But he definitely did hear a noise behind him... No, he wasn't going to look, it was a trick. "That's just another of Bear's snowballs."

"Well, it is—and it isn't," said Rabbit.

He tried to remember what his
three-legged grandfather had said about
avalanches. Oh yes, it's a good idea to
GET OUT OF THE WAY!

"Ah, that was it," panted Rabbit, and
jumped sideways.

"WHAT was it?" panted Wolf, and the
noise was so loud now that he finally
looked over his shoulder.

He didn't even have time to gasp.
A snowball the size of an
avalanche hit Wolf faster than a
train, and rolled him out on to the
thin ice of the lake. The ice cracked.

PLOP!

By the time Wolf had crawled ashore,
Rabbit was half a mile away.

Wolf snorted. Ouch. There was
something stuck up his nose. He sneezed.

Out popped the old, black, floppy carrot.
Wolf sniffed it. Ugh.

Still, he kind of liked the way it just sat
there.

SNIFF

"Hmmm. Maybe I'll try going vegetarian for a bit," said Wolf. "I'm sick of having my dinner run away from me at forty miles an hour."

68

Wolf gave the
carrot a bite.

BLUUUUUUHH!

Uggy uggy uggy! Bluuuuuuhh!
Wolf spat the old, black,
floppy carrot back into the lake.

69

He sighed, licked his huge, sharp teeth, and went home to dry off.

"Bear," said Rabbit, "why did you save me when I was so mean to you?"

"Because you gave me a carrot," said Bear.

"But it was an old, black, floppy carrot," replied Rabbit.

"It's the thought that counts," said Bear.

Rabbit blushed, and ran off.

Oh well, thought
Bear, I suppose
he's gone to eat. Or
poo. Or eat poo.

But he hadn't.

Back home, Rabbit pushed the body of his snowman until it rolled down his hill, and halfway up Bear's.

"Bear!" shouted Rabbit. "Help me push this snowball up your hill."

When they'd got it to the top, Rabbit panted, "It's a present... for your snowman."

They heaved the new head onto the body. Bear did most of the heaving, as Rabbit couldn't reach that high.

"Perfect," they said.

Bear carefully pushed two pine cones
into the head, for eyes.

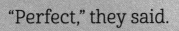

"Perfect," they said.

Rabbit picked up a curved stick, jumped as high as he could, and slapped a mouth on the snowman.

"Perfect," said Rabbit.

"Hmmmmm," said Bear.

The stick unstuck, and fell off.
Bear carefully put it back on
upside-down, so that it made a smile.

"Perfect," they said together.

"I'm afraid I lost the carrot that you gave me," said Bear.

Rabbit smiled, for the first time ever. It hardly hurt at all. He reached behind him. "Ta-dah!" Rabbit gave his best and brightest orange carrot to Bear. "For your snowman."

"No," said Bear.

"No?" asked Rabbit, shocked.

"For OUR snowman," said Bear as he carefully pushed the carrot nose into the snowman's head.

"Perfect," they said together.

"So," said Rabbit, happily. "Tomorrow we could meet up, and play, and..."

"Sorry," said Bear. "I'm really hungry, and I don't have any food. I'll have to go back to sleep until winter is over..."

Rabbit smiled. It was even easier the second time. He produced a honeycomb from behind his back. And a frozen salmon. And some delicious beetles' eggs.

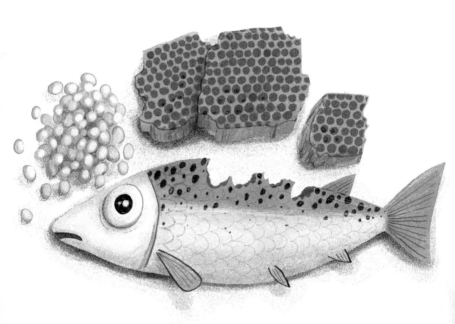

"But...but...this is just like the food I had!"
Bear said.

"It IS the food you had," said Rabbit. "I'm
sorry I stole it. You can have it all back."

"But then YOU
won't have any
food," said Bear.
"I don't think
I deserve any,"
said Rabbit, very
quietly.

"Well...look here, Rabbit," said Bear. "You don't like being a rabbit anyway. Why not stay in my cave, and be a bear, with me?"

"Perfect!" said Rabbit.

"Let's have a moonlight picnic to celebrate!" said Bear.

It was a long and lovely picnic. Bear had built up a wonderful appetite after sleeping half the winter, and Rabbit was, as usual, VERY, VERY hungry.

Rabbit looked out of the mouth of the warm cave, at the snowman glittering in the moonlight.

"He looks a little lonely, out there in the cold," said Rabbit.

"In the morning," murmured Bear,
"we can make him a friend."
And Rabbit and Bear fell asleep
together in their warm cave.

Outside, the snowman
smiled in the moonlight.

LOOK OUT FOR MORE
RABBIT & BEAR

FIND OUT WHAT HAPPENS NEXT IN:

A Pest in the Nest